W9-BIT-439

La Llorona
The Weeping Woman

La Llorona
The Weeping Woman

An Hispanic Legend told in Spanish and English

BY JOE HAYES

Illustrated by VICKI TREGO HILL
& MONA PENNYPACKER

The Tradition of Storytelling

UNDER A SHADING COTTONWOOD TREE in summer, or huddled close to the fireplace in winter, the Hispanic children of the Southwest once listened spellbound as their parents or grandparents told stories—ancient tales that were passed down through the years by word of mouth. There were stories of enchantment to open children's eyes in amazement and humorous tales to make them laugh. And there were many tales of witchcraft and ghostly happenings to send a chill down their spines. But the stories weren't told merely to entertain the children. Storytelling was a way for older ones to pass some wisdom and understanding on to the young.

Storytelling isn't practiced so much today, and many of the old tales have been forgotten. But one old story continues to work its spell upon the people— the story of La Llorona (lah yoh-RROH-nah). It is told throughout the Southwest and all over Mexico as well. No other story is better known or dearer to Hispanic Americans. *La Llorona* is truly the classic folk story of Hispanic America.

La Tradición de Contar Cuentos

BAJO LA SOMBRA DE UN ÁLAMO EN VERANO, o arrimado al fogón en invierno, los niños hispánicos del sudoeste en tiempos pasados escuchaban encantados mientras sus padres o abuelos les contaban historias— cuentos antiguos que se pasaban a través de los años de boca en boca. Había historias de encantamiento para abrirles los ojos asombrados a los niños y cuentos graciosos para hacerles reír. Había muchos relatos de brujerías y cosas espantosas para hacerles sentir escalofríos subir y bajar el espinazo. Pero se contaban las historias no sólo para divertir a los niños. Por medio de los cuentos, los mayores les pasaban algo de conocimiento y sabiduría a los niños.

La costumbre de contar historias no se practica tanto actualmente y muchos cuentos han sido olvidados. Pero una historia sigue encantando a la gente —la de La Llorona. Esta historia se cuenta por todo el sudoeste y por todo México también. Ninguna otra historia es más conocida ni más querida por los americanos hispánicos. *La Llorona* es verdaderamente la clásica historia folklórica de Norteamérica Hispánica.

THIS IS A STORY that the old ones have been telling to children for hundreds of years. It is a sad tale, but it lives strong in the memories of the people, and there are many who swear that it is true.

ESTA ES UNA HISTORIA que los viejitos han contado a los niños desde hace muchos siglos. Es una historia triste, pero se mantiene con fuerza en la memoria de la gente y hay muchos que juran que es la verdad.

LONG YEARS AGO in a humble little village there lived a fine-looking girl named María. Some say she was the most beautiful girl in the world! And because she was so beautiful, María thought she was better than everyone else.

HACE MUCHÍSIMOS AÑOS vivía en un pueblo humilde una bella muchacha llamada María. Dicen algunos que era la más hermosa de todo el mundo. Y como era tan linda, María se consideraba superior a la demás gente.

AS MARÍA GREW OLDER, her beauty increased. And her pride in her beauty grew too. When she was a young woman, she would not even look at the young men from her village. They weren't good enough for her!

"When I marry," María would say, "I'll marry the most handsome man in the world."

A MEDIDA QUE MARÍA CRECÍA, aumentaba su belleza. Y su altivez también aumentaba. No echaba ni una mirada a los jóvenes de su pueblo que la pretendían. No eran bastante guapos para ella.

—Cuando yo me case—, decía María—voy a casarme con el hombre más guapo del mundo.

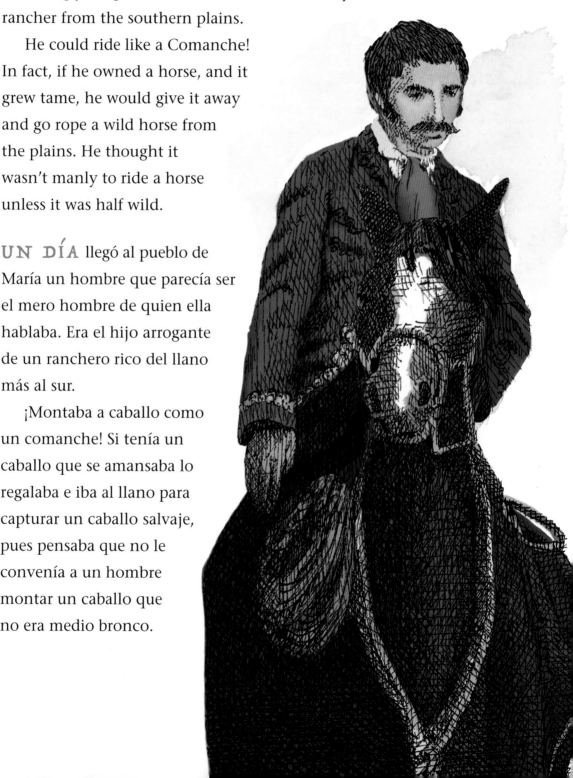

AND THEN ONE DAY, into María's village rode a man who seemed to be just the one she had been talking about. He was a dashing young ranchero—the son of a wealthy rancher from the southern plains.

He could ride like a Comanche! In fact, if he owned a horse, and it grew tame, he would give it away and go rope a wild horse from the plains. He thought it wasn't manly to ride a horse unless it was half wild.

UN DÍA llegó al pueblo de María un hombre que parecía ser el mero hombre de quien ella hablaba. Era el hijo arrogante de un ranchero rico del llano más al sur.

¡Montaba a caballo como un comanche! Si tenía un caballo que se amansaba lo regalaba e iba al llano para capturar un caballo salvaje, pues pensaba que no le convenía a un hombre montar un caballo que no era medio bronco.

HE WAS HANDSOME! And he could play the guitar and sing beautifully. María made up her mind—this was the man for her! She knew just the tricks to win his attention.

¡ERA GUAPÍSIMO! Tocaba la guitarra y cantaba bien. Y María se decidió que este era el hombre para ella. Tenía mañas para ganárselo.

IF THE RANCHERO SPOKE when they met on the pathway, she would turn her head away. When he came to her house in the evening to play his guitar and serenade her, she wouldn't even come to the window. She refused all his costly gifts.

The young man fell for her tricks. "That haughty girl María," he said to himself. "I can win her heart. That's the girl I'll marry."

SI EL RANCHERO LE HABLABA cuando se topaban en el sendero, María volteaba la cabeza. Cuando acudía por la tarde para tocar su guitarra y darle serenata a María, ella no iba a la ventana. Rechazaba los regalos costosos que el ranchero le enviaba.

El joven ranchero se enredó. —¡Esa engreída María—! se dijo a sí mismo—Yo puedo conquistar su corazón. Juro que me casaré con ella.

AND SO EVERYTHING TURNED OUT just as María planned. Before long, she and the ranchero became engaged and soon they were married.

At first, things were fine. They had two children and they seemed to be a happy family together.

Y TODO RESULTÓ como María había tramado. Dentro de poco María y el ranchero se comprometieron y luego se casaron. Al principio todo estaba bien. Tuvieron dos hijos y parecían una familia feliz.

BUT AFTER A FEW YEARS, the ranchero went back to the wild life of the prairies. He would leave town and be gone for months at a time. And when he returned home, it was only to visit his children. He seemed to care nothing for the beautiful María. He even talked of setting María aside and marrying a woman of his own wealthy class.

As proud as María was, of course she became very angry with the ranchero. She also began to feel anger toward her children, because he paid attention to them, but just ignored her.

PERO PASARON VARIOS AÑOS, y el ranchero volvió a la vida bárbara del llano. Se quedaba fuera del pueblo por meses. Cuando volvía a casa, era solamente para visitar a sus niños. No parecía sentir nada por la bella María. Hasta hablaba de dejar al lado a María para casarse con una mujer rica.

Siendo tan orgullosa, claro que María se enojaba mucho con el ranchero. Además se enojaba con sus hijos, pues el ranchero les mostraba mucho cariño mientras que a ella la desairaba.

ONE EVENING, as María was strolling with her two children on the shady pathway near the river, the ranchero came by in a carriage. An elegant woman sat on the seat beside him. He stopped and spoke to his children, but didn't even look at María. He whipped the horses on up the street.

UNA TARDE, cuando se paseaba María con sus niños por la alameda al lado del río, el ranchero pasó en un coche ligero. Una dama elegante estaba sentada a su lado. Paró el coche y saludó a sus hijos, pero no le dio ni un vistazo a María. Azotó a los caballos calle arriba.

WHEN SHE SAW THAT, a terrible rage filled María, and it all turned against her children. And, although it is sad to tell, the story says that in her anger María seized her two children and threw them into the river!

AL VER TODO ESO, María sintió una rabia terrible y toda la emoción se dirigió contra sus hijos. Y aunque de lástima decirlo, se cuenta que en su rabia María agarró a sus dos niños y los arrojó al río.

BUT AS THEY DISAPPEARED DOWN THE RIVER, she realized what she had done! She ran down the bank of the river, reaching out her arms to them. But they were long gone.

On and on ran María, driven by the fear that filled her heart, until finally she sank to the ground and lay still.

The next morning, a traveler brought word to the villagers that a beautiful woman lay dead on the bank of the river. That is where they found María, and they laid her to rest where she had fallen.

PERO AL VERLOS LLEVADOS RÍO ABAJO, María se dio cuenta de lo que había hecho. Echó a correr por la orilla del río extendiéndoles los brazos. Pero ya quedaron perdidos.

Corrió y corrió María, impulsada por el temor que llenó su corazón, hasta que se cayó rendida al suelo y quedó quieta.

A la mañana siguiente un viajero vio tendida en la orilla del río a una linda mujer muerta y contó la noticia a los del pueblo. Ahí encontraron a María y la enterraron donde había caído.

BUT FROM THE FIRST NIGHT she was in the grave, the villagers heard the sound of crying down by the river. At first they thought it was only the wind they were hearing. But when they listened more carefully, they heard words. "Aaaaaiiii...my children," a voice sobbed pitifully. "Where are my children?"

And they saw a woman walking up and down the bank of the river, dressed in a long white robe, the way they had dressed María for burial.

On many a dark night, they saw her walk the river bank. But more often, they would hear her cry for her children. And so they no longer spoke of her as María. They called her La Llorona (lah yoh-RROH-nah) —the weeping woman. And by that name she is known to this day.

PERO AQUELLA MISMA NOCHE la gente del pueblo oyeron algo como llantos cerca del río. Al principio, pensaron que era el viento. Pero al escuchar más bien oyeron palabras:—Aaaaaiiii...mis hijos—, lloraba una voz lastimosa. —¿Donde estan mis hijos...?

Vieron andar por la orilla del río a una mujer vestida en un manto largo y blanco, como el en que habían usado para vestir a María al enterrarla.

Muchas noches oscuras la veían recorrer la ribera. Pero más a menudo la oían llorar por sus niños. Así que dejaron de llamarle María y le llamaron "La Llorona." Y con este nombre es conocida hasta ahora.

AND THEY STILL WARN THE YOUNG ONES,

"When it grows dark, get inside the house. La Llorona may be about, looking for her children. Be careful! She might mistake you for one of her own children."

They tell of many children down through the years who have been chased by the crying ghost—and of some who have even been caught!

TODAVÍA ADVIERTEN A LOS CHICOS:—Cuando se oscurece, métanse dentro de la casa, que La Llorona puede estar por aquí buscando a sus hijos. ¡Ten cuidado! Te puede confundir a ti por uno de sus hijos.

Cuentan de muchos niños que han sido perseguidos por La Llorona. ¡Y de unos que han sido agarrados!

IS THE STORY REALLY TRUE? Who knows? Some claim that it is. Others say that it isn't. But the old ones still tell it to the children, just as they heard it themselves when they were young. And in the same way, the children who hear it today will some day tell it to their own children and grandchildren.

¿SERÁ CIERTA ESTA HISTORIA? ¿Quién sabe? Algunos sostienen que sí. Otros dicen que no. Pero los ancianos la cuentan a los niños, tal como la oyeron cuando ellos mismos eran niños. Y algun día los niños de hoy la contarán en la misma forma a sus propios hijos y nietos.

JOE HAYES is one of America's premier storytellers—
a nationally recognized teller of tales from the Hispanic,
Native American and Anglo cultures. His bilingual
Spanish-English tellings have earned him a distinctive
place among America's storytellers. His books and tapes
of Southwestern stories are popular nationwide.

Joe began sharing his stories in print in 1982. His
books have received the Arizona Young Readers Award,
The Land of Enchantment Children's Book Award, two
IPPY Awards, a Southwest Book Award and an Aesop
Accolade Award. His books have been on the Texas
Bluebonnet Award Master List three times.

VICKI TREGO HILL lives in El Paso, Texas where
she operates a design studio specializing in books. Her
work with Cinco Puntos Press has helped to establish
her reputation as one of the Southwest's finest book
illustrators and designers.

Vicki drew the original illustrations for the first
duotone edition of *La Llorona* in 1987. For this current
edition, she modified some of the original drawings
and drew several new ones. She asked her daughter,
MONA PENNYPACKER, to add color to these
illustrations. Mona, an artist in her own right, divides
her time between her fiber arts studio and art direction
for GoodHandArts.com. She is also the illustrator for
Joe Hayes' most recent book, *Ghost Fever*.

NOTE TO READERS AND STORYTELLERS
LA LLORONA

THIS STORY differs from most of the traditional tales that are retold for young readers in that many people believe it to be true, which makes it more a legend than a folktale. Its origin has provided much speculation. In recent decades some writers have related La Llorona to Malinche, the Native mistress of Hernán Cortés; if the historic connection were valid, it would certainly make the story a legend, but this interpretation seems to be primarily an attempt to put a political spin on the narrative. Other writers see the origin of La Llorona in the Aztec goddess Cihuacoatl, who was associated with water and, like La Llorona, would spirit people away. A comparison, if not a connection, with the Greek myth of Jason and Medea is obvious. Documented references to the crying woman date from 1550 in Mexico; and today La Llorona is universally known in that country. The story is familiar to many in the southwestern United States as well, and its range is steadily increasing as the Mexican immigrant community grows ever more widely dispersed throughout the country.

My version is largely based on things I heard about La Llorona when I was a boy in Arizona, with some of my own inventions thrown in, of course, such as the names of the characters. I also give the tale a more logical structure than it had in the renditions I heard in my youth, but I leave some loose threads untied for future speculation. I avoid telling the tale to children younger than nine or ten years; however, if younger children are familiar with the story from their own families, they sometimes insist on hearing it.

In the oral tradition, references to La Llorona fall into three categories: 1) vague warnings that she might be wandering about; 2) legendary tales that explain the origin of the crying ghost; and 3) anecdotes of encounters with her. I have incorporated the first two categories in my story. When I tell it, I encourage the children to share their own examples of the third type, both their own experiences and those they've heard about from members of their families and communities. The quantity of stories that results is impressive, and each one is presented as unquestionably true. When children ask me if I believe in La Llorona, I answer as I do whenever I'm asked about a story: I don't think the things I told you really did happen, but if you think about the story you can find a lot of truth in it.

—*JOE HAYES*

Visit us at www.cincopuntos.com
or call 1-800-566-9072

**Cover and book design by
Vicki Trego Hill of El Paso, Texas.
Illustrations by Mona Pennypacker
& Vicki Trego Hill. Special thanks
to Rose Hill and Ailbhe Aboud.**

La Llorona / The Weeping Woman. Copyright © 2004 by Joe Hayes. Illustrations copyright © 2004 by Vicki Trego Hill and Mona Pennypacker. All rights reserved. No part of this book may be used or reproduced in any manner whatsoever without written permission except in case of brief quotations for reviews. For information, write Cinco Puntos Press, 701 Texas, El Paso, TX 79901 or call at (915) 838-1625. Printed in Hong Kong.
FIRST EDITION 10 9 8 7 6 5
Library of Congress Cataloging-in-Publication Data. Hayes, Joe. La llorona = The weeping woman : an Hispanic legend told in Spanish and English / by Joe Hayes ; illustrated by Vicki Trego Hill and Mona Pennypacker.— 3rd ed., enl. p. cm   Summary: Retells, in parallel English and Spanish text, the traditional Hispanic American tale of a proud and beautiful woman who, in a fit of jealousy, commits a terrible act and then cannot stop weeping for it, even after she is dead. ISBN-13: 978-0-938317-39-5 / ISBN-10: 0-938-31739-3 (paperback) (alk. paper)
1. Llorona (Legendary character)—Legends. [1. Llorona (Legendary character)—Legends. 2. Folklore—Southwest, New. 3. Folklore—Mexico. 4. Spanish language materials—Bilingual.] I. Title: Weeping woman. II. Hill, Vicki Trego, ill. III. Pennypacker, Mona, ill. IV. Title. PZ74.1.H34 2004   398.2'0979'02—dc22   2004013368

Printed in Hong Kong by Morris Printing